By Order of His Majesty, King Claude

Written by Quentin Flynn

Illustrated by Richard Hoit

Contents

NELSON
CENGAGE Learning™
For learning solutions, visit **cengage.com.au**

Meet the Characters

King Claude IV

The ruler of Montpelliovia.

Sir Montgomery-Quince

The lord chamberlain.

Lady Sally

The royal wardrobier.

Joe

A cafe owner.

Lollipop Ladies

A delegation.

Field-Marshals

Commanders of the army.

Dear Reader

I once went to a shop in a smart area of town. I was nicely dressed, and the shop assistants were all very attentive and helpful. When I went back the next day, I'd been working in the garden, and I had my dirty old gardening clothes on.

Everyone ignored me! It's funny how what you wear changes people's ideas about how they should behave towards you.

Quentin Flynn
Author

Around the Montpelliovian Palace

1. The palace
2. The palace gates
3. The pedestrian crossing
4. Joe's Dinery

1 A Royal Lunch

His Majesty King Claude IV, ruler of the small kingdom of Montpelliovia, poked at his royal lunch with a silver fork. Even with a dressing of the rarest grated truffles, the kingdom's rosiest lobster, finest caviar and plumpest oysters were unappetising.

Even the cup of kopi luwak coffee, ground from the world's most expensive coffee beans, didn't inspire him. He was bored with royal food. He felt like a bacon sandwich and a fizzy drink.

He put his fork down and twiddled glumly with a lobster leg. Then he pushed the specks of caviar around his plate until they made letters.

"B-O-R- …"

"Is everything all right with your lunch, sire?" came a voice.

"Yes, it's fine, thank you," said King Claude IV, with a noble wave of his lobster leg. He tried to smile at Sir Montgomery-Quince, his lord chamberlain. It was the chamberlain's job to wear white gloves, remind the king of his meetings and put plates of regal food in front of the king three times a day. "Splendid, as always," the king sighed.

King Claude IV ate a single speck of caviar. He screwed up his face as the tiny fish egg burst in his mouth. To take his mind off the taste, he imagined a streaky bacon rasher pressed between two thick slices of bread. In his mind, the sandwich floated off a plate and headed for his mouth. But this only made him feel even more miserable.

Then it occurred to him that he was the king, and he could do pretty much as he wished without getting into trouble. As long as he didn't invade next-door kingdoms or fire cannons for fun after dark or play marbles with the crown jewels, nobody would tell him off. Actually, nobody had told him off when he had done those things last week. But he could tell from the faint looks of disapproval on the faces of his royal field marshals, neighbouring lords and ladies, and the castle jeweller that he should probably find other ways to amuse himself.

"I'm just nipping out," he said to Sir Montgomery-Quince, pushing his plate away and standing up.

"Shall I order the royal grooms to brush the horses and bring the carriage around to the front?

Or do you want the royal limousine?" asked the lord chamberlain with a bow.

"No, thanks," replied King Claude IV. "I'm going for a walk."

A faint look of horror crossed Sir Montgomery-Quince's face. "Would you like me to brush your finest English shoes first?" he inquired.

King Claude IV looked down at his black slippers, embroidered in silk with the regal crest of arms. "These will do fine," he declared.

Sir Montgomery-Quince suppressed a gasp. "As you wish, your majesty," he murmured.

The king padded out of the royal dining room. He scuffed his way down a marble staircase. Taking the royal honour guard marching up and down the palace's parade ground by surprise, he headed for the palace gates.

The soldiers at the gates saluted as soon as they saw the king. The king nodded and breezed past.

On one of his royal trips to wave at his loyal subjects from the window of his limousine, he'd seen a cafe across the road.

"I bet they have bacon sandwiches," he thought to himself. He was so caught up in his dreamy visions of floating bacon sandwiches that he didn't see the lollipop lady at the pedestrian crossing a few paces down the road. He strode into the traffic, oblivious to the squealing of brakes, skidding of tyres and the humble apologies from the drivers – and the lollipop sign being waved in his direction. "And probably fizzy drinks, too," he thought to himself, reaching the other side of the road.

2 A Royal Visitor

King Claude IV's arrival in the cafe, which was called Joe's Dinery, caused an uproar. The patrons, who were mostly taxi drivers with tweed caps and road workers with orange hard hats and vests, stared at the king with their mouths open.

Then the cafe exploded with the sounds of scraping chairs, clattering knives and forks, and cups rattling on saucers. The diners hurried to their feet and bowed while trying to swallow whatever food was half-chewed in their mouths.

A small man wearing a knotted handkerchief on his head and an apron with the words "Your Opinion Wasn't in the Recipe!" ran out from behind the counter. Despite his rotund stomach, he bowed obsequiously.

Joe's Dinery
Bacon Sandwich
Bacon 'n' eggs
Fizzy Drinks
Your Opinion Wasn't in the Recipe!
S

"Sire, I am your humble servant, Joe," he said, addressing his knees. "If you've come about the tax bill I've been meaning to pay for the last three months, I'm very, very sorry, your majesty. I will never, ever be late again. Honest."

"Actually, I'd like some lunch," said the king brightly. "Do you have a spare table?"

With some effort, Joe straightened up. "At once, your majesty," he cried, shooing away a group of road workers from a table of half-eaten sandwiches. He cleared all the dishes and crusts, and gave the tabletop a rub with his apron. He drew back the plastic chair.

"Your table awaits, sire," said Joe.

King Claude IV sat at the table and looked at the menu above the counter. He spied exactly what he wanted. "I'd like a bacon …"

But Joe was talking to his knees again. "Sire, do not trouble yourself with our humble menu," he said. "I shall make you something special myself." He backed through the crowd until he bumped into the counter. Then he turned and scurried into the kitchen.

The sounds of barked orders, clattering saucepans and furious chopping came from the kitchen. Several waiters with shopping lists darted out the front door of Joe's Dinery, pausing only to bow nervously at the king before racing out into the street. King Claude IV realised he was the only one sitting in the entire cafe.

He turned and looked over his shoulder at the taxi drivers and road workers standing behind him. "Carry on!" he beamed. But, instead of resuming their meals, they shuffled awkwardly past the king's table, doffing their tweed caps and orange hard hats, and headed for the door. No one wanted to be caught eating macaroni cheese with the wrong macaroni-cheese fork or slurping pea and ham soup from the wrong side of a soup plate while the king was watching.

Eventually, the waiters returned, with brown paper parcels under their arms. More shouting and clattering came from the kitchen. And, after about twenty minutes, which even to the king

seemed like a long time to sizzle strips of streaky bacon, Joe came out with a large oval plate with what looked like a hubcap over the top.

"I'm sorry I don't have any silverware to present your majesty's lunch on," said Joe. "But I have found some stainless steel knives and forks instead of the white plastic ones we usually use here."

The king was about to ask why anyone eating a bacon sandwich would need a knife and fork, when Joe whipped off the hubcap from the plate.

"Bon appétit!" he said, and backed away from the king's table.

King Claude IV stared at the dish before him in abject disappointment.

Lobster.

Caviar.

Oysters.

He wrinkled his nose and sniffed. He sighed. There was no mistaking the musty, chocolatey aroma of freshly grated truffles. With a sad look, he picked up a spiny lobster leg and speared a single blob of caviar.

3 Military Strategy

The king politely thanked Joe for the lunch he had prepared. He said he was sorry for having to return to the palace to attend to some urgent matters of state that meant he couldn't eat more than one tiny speck of caviar.

The mere fact that King Claude IV had eaten at his cafe was more than enough for Joe. In fact, after the king left to trudge back to the palace, Joe got a photographer to come and take softly lit portraits of the king's leftovers, which he intended to frame and display on the walls of his cafe.

"Your majesty," nodded Sir Montgomery-Quince when the king got back to the palace. He tapped his watch. "I trust you haven't forgotten your meeting with the Montpelliovian army field marshals in half an hour."

“Bother,” muttered King Claude IV. “I had forgotten. I’d better go and change into my supreme Montpelliovian commander’s uniform.” He sighed. The field marshals always seemed to take more notice of his clever military schemes when he had his full dress uniform on. A tunic covered in medals and a sabre on his hip made all the difference.

Lady Sally, the wardrobier, bustled in and out of the king’s ensuite wardrobe. She laid out sashes, garters, medals, fur-lined army coats and freshly polished boots. The king sat on his bed. He was hungry and feeling very sorry for himself. Finally, he couldn’t stand it any longer.

“All I wanted was a bacon sandwich!” he wailed. “And a fizzy drink!”

Lady Sally, who was not used to hearing much from the king apart from spur-of-the-moment decisions such as whether he wanted a bright yellow or the bright green handkerchief jauntily folded into his jacket pocket, looked startled. “I beg your pardon, your majesty?”

King Claude IV sulkily related the tale of his trip to Joe’s Dinery. “It’s not fair,” he said. “All the other diners got to eat what they wanted. I shouldn’t be treated any differently.”

“The clothes we wear do tend to reflect who we are,” said the wardrobier. She nodded towards the king’s royal robes. “If your majesty goes to Joe’s Dinery dressed as a king, he should expect to be treated like a king.”

“And what if I went to Joe’s Dinery dressed

as a taxi driver or a road worker?" muttered the king stubbornly. "Would I be treated differently then?"

"Well …" started Lady Sally.

"What a good idea," smiled the king, immediately pleased with his clever plan. "I'm promoting you to chief majestic disguisier."

The wardrobier nodded her head nervously. "As you wish, sire," she said. "But I don't really think …"

"What are you waiting for?" interrupted the king. "I need an orange hard hat and a vest. And get me a tweed cap, too, just in case."

The newly appointed chief majestic disguisier bowed and slipped out of the royal bedroom. King Claude twiddled with the shiny buttons and gold braid on the grand military uniform laid out on his bed.

King Claude IV's heart sank when he saw the gloomy faces of the field marshals gathered around the royal plotting table. Their steely eyes and impressive uniforms intimidated him, even though, being the supreme commander, he was technically in charge. He knew he shouldn't have invaded the neighbouring kingdom of Vipernum, but he had been bored. Besides, his cousin, the Vipernian crown prince, had beaten him in a game of snakes and ladders that week and he wasn't happy about it.

"Can't we just retreat?" he said, after the field marshals explained how the Vipernian forces had surrounded the well-dressed but unenthusiastic sabre-rattling Montpelliovian soldiers.

“As long as he is wearing the proud uniform of a Montpelliovian, a soldier from your army will never retreat!” boomed one of the field marshals.

“Well, that leaves us in a spot of bother then,” said the king, expertly summing up the complex military situation. He looked around the table, hoping one of the field marshals would come up with a brilliantly cunning plan. They just adjusted their monocles and medals and looked back at their supreme Montpelliovian commander, awaiting orders.

The king’s highly tuned sense of military strategy deserted him. It’s because I’m hungry, he thought to himself. His eyes glazed over and an image of a bacon sandwich threatened to ruin his military focus. He shook the image from his head and confidently went to plan B.

“Carry on!” ordered King Claude IV.

Later that day, the king sat on the edge of his bed. He wondered if he should just apologise to the Vipernian crown prince and invite him over for a game of snap or pick-up sticks. Then there was a knock on the king's door.

"Ooh, maybe that's my chief majestic disguisier!" he exclaimed. He jumped off the bed and opened the door.

"Oh," he said. "It's you."

"Sire," said Sir Montgomery-Quince. "There is a delegation from the Grand and Ancient Union of Lollipop Ladies here to see you," he murmured.

"Right," said the king. As their royal patron, King Claude IV knew the ladies from the union. In their sinister white coats and sunhats, they were one of the few groups that intimidated him even more than the field marshals.

4 The Lollipop Ladies

"Something needs to be done!" declared the chief organiser of the Grand and Ancient Union of Lollipop Ladies, whose senior members were sitting around the royal plotting table, fixing the king with withering gazes.

"It does!" agreed King Claude IV, with a nod of his head. He kept glancing at the door, hoping one of his field marshals would reappear with some news of the Vipernian campaign that would need his immediate attention.

"Every day, our members see incidents where drivers are not paying attention," continued the chief organiser. "And there have been escalations."

"Escalations!" repeated the king, exhaling seriously. "Whatever next?"

STOP
STOP
STOP
STOP

"Absolutely," continued the chief organiser, above the murmurs of her colleagues. "We have even had reports of pedestrians not behaving themselves properly in areas under our trafficarial authority." She sat back and fixed the king with a quivering eyebrow.

"Really?" said the king.

"Yes!" snapped the chief organiser. "It appears some people think that simply because they are wearing a crown, regal robes and silk slippers, they are above the law."

King Claude IV, who was surprised to learn that someone else in Montpelliovia had a crown, regal robes and silk slippers, shook his head at the foolishness of some people, especially those who felt they were above the law simply because of what they were wearing.

"Something does need to be done," agreed the king. He looked at the lollipop ladies, hoping one of them would drop a hint about what exactly that was. All he saw was a wall of stony faces.

Fortunately, at that moment, he heard the front door of the palace click shut and saw his chief majestic disguisier hurrying past, carrying "You Need It, We Tweed It" and "Never-Knocked Safety Stuff" shopping bags.

The king stood up and addressed the lollipop ladies in a stately voice. "You have my full support for doing what needs to be done," he rumbled. "Carry on!"

The king was so excited at the sight of the hard hats, safety vests and tweed caps that he decided, right there and then, that he would simply have to sleep in his new disguise that night.

He ignored the royal shortie pyjamas neatly folded on his regal pillows, pulled on his bright orange vest and climbed into bed. And when he woke up the next morning, he was delighted to find that everything was perfectly crumpled. Clearly, he thought, that was what real taxi drivers and road workers did to get that authentic look.

"There's only one thing better than bacon sandwiches for lunch," said the king, popping his hard hat on and checking his new look in the royal mirror, "and that's bacon sandwiches for breakfast!" He scurried downstairs.

"Oi, you!" came Sir Montgomery-Quince's stentorian voice. King Claude IV turned around to find the lord chamberlain frowning at him. "The tradesperson's entrance is around the back. Get out of here this instant!"

The king doffed his orange hard hat. Allowing himself a regal chuckle, he scuttled out the front door. He crossed the parade ground and walked to the palace gates, where the two soldiers on duty greeted him with a sniff.

The king strolled out the gates and stepped off the kerb. He was quite unprepared for the torrent of abuse and honking of horns that greeted him as soon as he started to cross the road.

He stepped back hurriedly, resolving to consult his dictionary for the meaning of "nincompoop", "buffoon" and "noodle-head".

Just then, the lollipop lady to his left blew her whistle and, once the traffic stopped, she led a group of children across the road.

"So that's what should be done," said the king. "Jolly good idea." He walked down to the crossing and waited patiently for the lollipop lady to exercise her trafficarial authority once more.

OOKS
Joe's Dinery
OPEN
STOP

Inside Joe's Dinery, the morning rush was in full swing. King Claude IV went up to the counter and nodded at Joe, who was wearing the same knotted handkerchief and apron as the day before.

"Top of the morning, my good man," started King Claude IV. "I'd like a bacon …"

"Oi!" came a chorus of voices from behind him. "Join the queue, mate." The king looked around to see a sea of thumbs jabbing towards the back of a long line of hungry customers.

"How exciting," thought the king. "I've never had to stand in line before!"

5 A Bacon Sandwich

Ten minutes later, King Claude IV found himself feeling fulfilled and happy at last. In his left hand, he carried a bottle of fizzy drink and in his right, a plastic plate bearing two slabs of white bread enclosing a cluster of streaky strips of bacon.

He found himself a spare chair at a table of road workers and politely inquired if he might grace their table with his esteemed presence.

"Hrrmph," replied one of the men, chomping on a sandwich.

"Grrmph," added another, slurping a cup of tea.

The king sat down and savoured every morsel of his bacon sandwich, enjoying the parry and

BURP!
S

thrust of the witty conversation swirling around him. He washed his breakfast down with a swig of delightfully gassy fizzy drink and, anxious not to offend local customs, followed that with a gigantic, rumbling burp. The eyebrows raised in silent approval around the table meant more to King Claude IV than the smartest salute he ever got from a palace guard.

"Oi, you!" bellowed Sir Montgomery-Quince as the king strolled back into the palace, his veins happily coursing with saturated fats, sugary syrup and vast quantities of fibre-free carbohydrate. "What part of 'tradesperson's entrance' didn't I make clear?"

The king strolled over and winked at the lord chamberlain. "It's me," he whispered. "King Claude IV." He took off his orange hard hat so Sir Montgomery-Quince could get a better look at his face.

"I … I … er, sorry, your majesty," stammered the lord chamberlain, after peering at the face in front of him. "I didn't recognise you without your crown, robes and royal slippers."

"Excellent," beamed the king.

"Don't forget you are due to consult with the Montpelliovian army field marshals at ten-thirty," muttered Sir Montgomery-Quince, trying to act normally. He was wondering what was going on.

King Claude IV looked at the clock on the palace wall. He'd had such a good time at Joe's Dinery he'd lost track of time. It was already ten o'clock.

"Bother," he sighed. "I'd better go upstairs and extricate myself from my cleverly constructed disguise."

The chief majestic disguisier bustled in and out of the king's ensuite wardrobe, laying out the usual selection of sashes, garters, medals, fur-lined army coats and freshly polished boots. The king sat glumly on the bed, surveying the unworn shortie pyjamas still on his pillow. He wasn't looking forward to his meeting with the field marshals. There were only so many times a king could fall back on the "carry on" strategy before some disaster or another ruined everything.

“My morning was so nice up until now,” he moaned. “It’s amazing what a difference a change of clothes makes.”

“It is indeed,” agreed Lady Sally. “As you’ve seen, people do treat each other differently depending on what they’re wearing. Which is silly, because it really shouldn’t matter …”

“That’s it!” cried the king, thumping his pillow and sending the pyjamas flying. “You’re brilliant.”

The chief majestic disguisier wasn’t sure whether the king was referring to her or himself. But she had her suspicions.

6 A Brilliant Plan

"What's the least threatening and most unmilitary thing you can think of?" said the king, pacing up and down in front of the royal plotting table.

A few of the field marshals toyed with the idea of saying "a king", but before they could mutter anything, King Claude IV continued to outline his brilliant military strategy.

"Exactly!" he said, although no one had replied. "Soldiers wearing shortie pyjamas!" He looked around at the field marshals triumphantly. "If no soldier wearing a Montpelliovian uniform will ever retreat, we need to supply each and every one of them with a pair of shortie pyjamas and allow them to return to a heroes' welcome with their dignity intact."

The field marshals looked at each other, wondering who would be the first to point out the incongruity of adults in shortie pyjamas keeping their dignity intact.

"But …" started one of the field marshals.

"But they mustn't throw out their military uniforms or their sabres," added the king. "I need them for something else."

"But …" repeated the field marshal.

"I know just what you're thinking," said the king. "Where are we going to find a thousand pairs of shortie pyjamas at short notice? I've already thought of that. I'd like to introduce the new supreme Montpelliovian commander."

The king beamed broadly at the thought of his superbly crafted plan to rescue his troops from the Vipernians and rescue himself from these dreary meetings with his field marshals. He beckoned Lady Sally, who had been waiting quietly outside the room.

“There should be more than enough upstairs in the king’s ensuite wardrobe,” she explained. “His majesty likes the green spotty ones and the ones with cartoon characters.”

After he left his supreme Montpelliovian commander and her field marshals to flesh out the finer details of the superb military plan, King Claude phoned his cousin to tell him that all the Vipernian forces needed to do was get a few garden hoses and set about sprinkling the Montpelliovian soldiers in their new shortie pyjama uniforms. That would be sure to send them running home without further incident. He also asked if his cousin would like to come over for a game of snap.

Then he called the Grand and Ancient Union of Lollipop Ladies and told them that something was indeed being done, and they should expect their new uniforms and quite possibly some leftover sabres, too, within a day or two.

This, he assured them, would solve the problem of impatient motorists and crown-wearing pedestrians. And, he added, his new supreme commander was so good, she would be taking over as their new patron as of today.

7 All the Difference

King Claude IV, ruler of Montpelliovia, laid back on his bed and, because it had been a busy few hours since breakfast, he thought about an urgent matter of state. Lunch.

He wondered if it was a good idea to have two bacon sandwiches in a day, but on reflection, decided that even a king should watch what he ate once in a while. Besides, he thought, sitting up and glancing at his reflection in the mirror, he'd changed into his royal costume for the meeting with the field marshals, and that meant that everyone would treat him differently if he went back to Joe's Dinery. That would be no fun.

"Anyway, there has to be some advantages to having a crown, fur-lined cape and embroidered silk slippers in your wardrobe," he said to himself. He wondered if the imposter that the lollipop ladies had reported yesterday had been caught yet. King Claude IV stood up and patted the orange safety vest and hard hat on his pillow. He would use them again one day soon.

But right now, he had something else on his mind.

"I hope they've got lobsters, oysters and caviar today," he thought hungrily, heading for the royal dining room. "And a dusting of truffles as dressing. After all, a dressing makes all the difference."

“After all,
a dressing makes
all the difference.”